2 498333 21

D1645830

Bertrams	13/01/2020
	£6.99
REN	

THE TERRIFIC
BIRTHDAY
RECIPE

Katy Hudson

raintree

a Capstone company — publishers for children

Raintree is an imprint of Capstone Global Library Limited, a company incorporated in England and Wales having its registered office at 264 Banbury Road, Oxford, OX2 7DY – Registered company number: 6695582

www.raintree.co.uk
myorders@raintree.co.uk

Copyright © Katy Hudson 2020
The moral rights of the proprietor have been asserted.

All rights reserved.

ISBN 978 1 4747 7807 7

A full catalogue record for this book is available from the British Library.

Printed and bound in India.

Designer:
Kay Fraser

For my perfectly
imperfect daughter,
Mabel.–K.H.

Beaver had always liked everything
to be done properly.

Every project he took on
was done **CAREFULLY**.

THOUGHTFULLY.

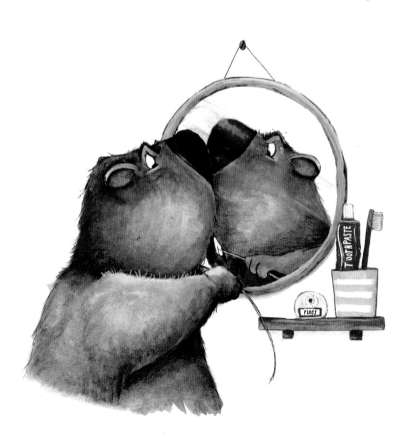

And as Beaver saw it . . .

PERFECTLY.

Beaver's birthday was the following day,
and his latest project had taken some time to plan.

It would have a chocolate layer, a carrot layer, a strawberry
layer, another chocolate layer, chocolate swirls, caramel,
icing, sprinkles and lots and lots of candles.

It would be the PERFECT birthday cake.

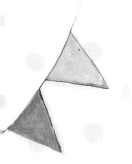

"It's incredible!" said Tortoise, the next day.

"It's ever so big," tweeted Bird. "Will you have enough time to make it all by yourself?"

"Of course not! We'll all help!" offered Rabbit brightly.

"Actually, I have a very specific recipe – " started Beaver.

"BRILLIANT!" interrupted Rabbit. "It will be so much fun to do it together. And for your birthday too!"

But Beaver had planned his cake very carefully. What if his friends didn't read his recipe properly?

As it turns out, Beaver was right to have concerns. On the recipe, "two carrots" looked like "two hundred carrots" to Rabbit.

"Too many carrots!" cried Beaver.

"OOPS!" said Rabbit.

The carrot cake layer
was ruined.

Squirrel could fetch ingredients faster than
Beaver could read them out.

 However, she was too fast at getting
them in the mixing bowl . . .

Tortoise worked carefully and slowly.
Maybe a little TOO slowly . . .

Edible stars

"Tortoise! It's dripping everywhere!"
panicked Beaver. "This will never do."

Bird felt it was only right to add
her family's "secret ingredient"
to the chocolate layers.

"ARGHHHH! What have you done?" cried Beaver.
"The secret ingredient is marshmallows!"

As the last candle was lit, Beaver's friends happily cheered their work.

"What a perfect cake for you!" clapped Squirrel.

"It took all day, but it was worth it," said Rabbit. **"HAPPY BIRTHDAY!"**

And that was when Beaver **SNAPPED!**

"This is the **UGLIEST**,
most **DISGUSTING** cake
I have ever seen!" he yelled.

"None of you followed
my very clear recipe."

"You used up all my ingredients, and it took you all day.
I will have to start all over again – ALONE!"

While his friends slept,
Beaver worked.
He whisked and he stirred.

He balanced and he spread.

He twirled and he decorated.
Until finally, there it was . . .

. . . his **PERFECT** birthday cake.
Perfectly baked, perfectly iced
and perfectly balanced.

And yet it was not perfect at all.
He looked around the empty
picnic blanket and sniffed away a sob.

Then **ANOTHER** and **ANOTHER**
and **ANOTHER** sob – until he couldn't stop.

His poor friends couldn't sleep through all the sobbing.

"I missed my entire birthday trying to make everything perfect, and nothing is perfect at all," Beaver said. "My friends didn't even turn up to my party."

"Only because we were
sleeping. It is the middle of
the night," comforted Rabbit.
"Now come on, off to bed."

The following day, Beaver's
friends threw him a party.
The decorations were WONKY,
the lemonade was SOUR
and the cake was STALE,
with the odd pickled worm in it.

It was not at all what Beaver
had planned, but it was the best
birthday he had ever had.
It was, in fact, perfect.

HAPPY BIRTHDAY, BEAVER!